Continuemos CD-ROM
for Spanish Language Study

User's Guide
Windows® and Macintosh® **CD-ROM**

Houghton Mifflin Company

Credits

Sponsoring Editor:	Roland Hernandez
Editorial Technology Manager:	Laurel Miller
Content Providers:	Lois Grossman, Tufts University
	Eda Henao,
	Borough of Manhattan College
	Steven T. Budge,
	Mesa Community College
Software Producer:	Sarah Tasker
Software Developed by:	InterWrite
Marketing Manager:	Tina Crowley Desprez

Visit Houghton Mifflin College Division on the Web: http://college.hmco.com.

Contents

Welcome to the Continuemos CD-ROM for Spanish Language Study

This educational software contains materials that supplement each chapter of the **Continuemos** textbook, by Jarvis, Lebredo, and Mena-Ayllón. The goal of this multimedia CD-ROM is to provide additional interactive practice and to reinforce video and main text content in a self-paced environment. Each chapter includes all or some combination of these five segments of learning content:

- *Vocabulary*
- *Grammar*
- *Application*
- *Video*
- *Games* (crosswords, timed word searches, space invader word association games, word completion maze games)

Multiple, varied question types test student knowledge of chapter subject matter:

- Fill-in exercises
- Drag and drop activities that include matching, sorting, ordering, or labeling tasks
- True or False questions
- Multiple choice activities
- Short answer or essay questions

- Record-your-response exercises (in response to audio, visual, or text questions)

In addition, the CD-ROM program is integrated with *Smarthinking*, Houghton Mifflin's live, online, text-specific tutoring service for students.

Program Requirements

The **Continuemos** CD-ROM for Spanish Language Study requires that you have the following applications to view the files supplied:

Microsoft Internet Explorer 5.x or higher (not included) or Netscape Navigator 4.7 or higher (not included)
Microsoft Word or WordPad for Windows (not included) or Simple Text (not included)

Minimum System Requirements

Windows:
WIN 95 (with latest updates) and later, including WIN XP
64 MB of available RAM, 128 MB recommended
Hard disk space or removable discs for saving recordings, notes and reports
4X+ CD-ROM
Pentium Processor
Monitor Resolution: 600x800 minimum, 1024 x 768 recommended
Recommended color setting or palette: 32bit or True color
Microphone

Macintosh:
Mac OS 8.6 (with Carbon Lib) and later, including OSX
128 MB of available RAM
Hard disk space or removable discs for saving recordings, notes and reports
4X+ CD-ROM
PowerMac or PowerPC
Monitor Resolution: 600x800 minimum, 1024 x 768 recommended
Recommended color setting or palette: thousands of colors
Microphone

Launching Continuemos

Windows:
1. Insert the CD-ROM into your disk drive.
2. Double click **My Computer** on your desktop.
3. Double click on the **Continuemos** CD-ROM icon in My Computer.
4. Double click on the Continuemos Flash icon to launch the CD-ROM.

Macintosh:
1. Insert the CD-ROM into your disk drive.
2. Double click on the **Continuemos** CD-ROM icon on your desktop.
3. Double click on the Continuemos Flash icon to launch the CD-ROM.

How to Use this HMCo World Language CD-ROM

<u>Welcome Screen</u>
The **Welcome** screen includes an overview of the CD-ROM and links to **About** and **Help** information. The **Welcome** screen also includes a login. You will need to login each time you use the CD-ROM to personalize the program.

If you would like to e-mail work completed in a CD-ROM study session to your professor (or anyone else), include the e-mail address at the bottom of the login. This e-mail address will be automatically entered when you launch your e-mail application from the program exercise screens.

Main Menu

When you click the login button on the **Welcome** screen, you will be taken to the **Main Menu**. The **Main Menu** has a navigation bar on the top right that allows you to go to the **Chapter Menu** as well as various supplemental sections of the CD-ROM, such as **Reference** (discussed later), **WWW** (which gives you access to the *Continuemos* website and the *Smarthinking* online tutorial program), **About**, and **Help**.

The primary navigation in the CD-ROM is the **Main Menu**, shown in the Personal Digital Assistant (PDA) on the left in the image on the next page. Mouse-over a chapter in the **Main Menu** PDA to see the core segments within each chapter. The segments within each chapter appear in a window immediately to the right of the **Main Menu** PDA.

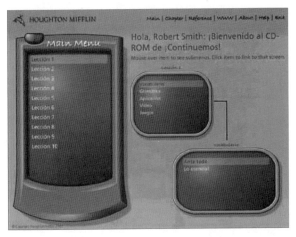

If you mouse-over the segment titles in the segment menu shown in the center of the screen, lesson topics within that segment are revealed in a smaller window below.

To go to the **Chapter Menu**, click on the chapter title in the **Main Menu** PDA.

To go to the first exercise in either a segment or a specific lesson topic, simply mouse-over the chapter and segment until the desired item is revealed, then click to jump to the first exercise in the chosen area.

Chapter Menu

Clicking on a chapter title in the **Main Menu** PDA, or clicking on
Chapter in the top navigation bar, takes you to the **Chapter
Menu**. The **Chapter Menu** works similarly to the **Main Menu**. You
mouse-over items to reveal lesson topics and then click to go to the
first exercise in the highlighted item.

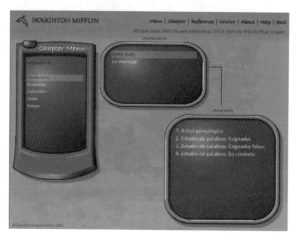

In the illustration above, the **Chapter Menu** PDA shows the
segments within a chapter. Immediately to the right is a small
window, showing the topics available in the highlighted segment. On

8

the bottom right is another small screen with the exercises included in the chosen and highlighted topic.

Exercise Screen

The exercise screens are reached from either the **Main Menu** or the **Chapter Menu**. The exercises are pop-up screens that appear on top of the menus. At any point, you can return to any menu by clicking the menu behind the exercise screen or clicking the desired menu in the top navigation bar.

The top of the exercise screen has a title. This title tells you what chapter segment you are in. You can jump to the next exercise or topic by clicking the arrows to the right of **Topic** or **Exercise**. To go to a previous exercise or topic, click the left backward pointing arrows.

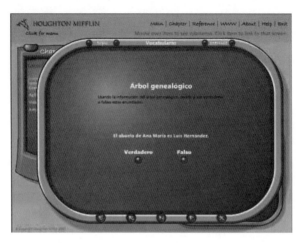

At the bottom of the exercise screen there are several buttons. Hold your mouse over these buttons to see a longer label describing their function.

> • **E** button: launches your default e-mail application. If you do not have a default e-mail application on your computer, you will have to install and set one up to use this function.
> • **R** button: opens up your **Progress Report**. This report reflects what you have accomplished so far in your CD-ROM study session.
> • **N** button: pops up a blank page, allowing you to take notes from within the program.

- **P** button: prints the current screen.
- **X** button: exits the exercise screen. To exit the program, click **Exit** in the navigation bar at the top of the page.

Progress Report

The **Progress Report** can be launched from any exercise screen by clicking the **R** button. The **Progress Report** lists all exercises in the chapter. For the exercises you have worked on, it shows the number of questions completed within an exercise, the number of attempts you've taken to complete each exercise, your score, and your answers to open-ended questions (by clicking on the **Data** button). From the **Progress Report**, you can return to any exercise for further practice by clicking the exercise title in the center column of the report.

The displayed **Progress Report** screen can be printed out by clicking the **P** button at the bottom the **Progress Report** screen. This program prints one screen at time so you may have to print, scroll down, and print again to print the entire report.

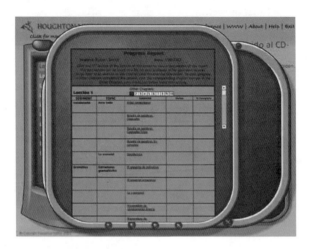

To print the full **Progress Report**, e-mail it, or save it as a file,
click the **T** button at the bottom of the Progress Report screen. This
will launch a new screen with a text version of the report.

Progress Report Text Output
The **Progress Report Text** screen is a complete version of the
Progress Report that can be saved to a file. It can then be easily
printed, e-mailed as an attachment to your professor, or saved for
your own records.

To save your **Progress Report** to a file:
• Select the text you want to save if it is not already selected.
• Copy the selected text   (Windows: Control+C; MAC: Command +C)
• Click the **S** (**Save**) button at the bottom of the screen and follow the prompts to save the report to a file.

To launch your e-mail application, click the **E** button at the bottom of the **Progress Report Text** screen.

Reference

Clicking the **Reference** label in the top navigation bar launches the **Reference** section of the CD. The reference section launches in a Web browser. Click an item in the left menu of the **Reference** section to jump to the desired reference material. Search reference material by using the **Find** button in your browser's top navigation bar. Most reference entries also have jump menus at the top of the document, allowing you to jump to document sections.

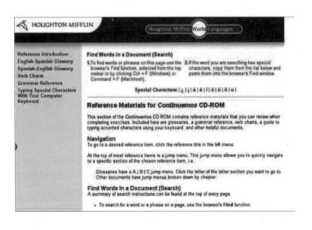

Games

This CD-ROM also includes a range of games to reinforce chapter lessons. These games include Crossword Puzzles and Word Searches, as well as Word Association Space Invader games, and Word Completion Maze games.

Crossword Puzzle: Clues are included for words that run both across and down (click on the corresponding button to see them).

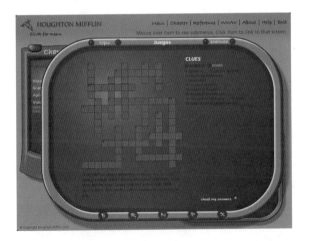

To enter your answer, click on the box associated with the number of the clue, then enter the letters of the word by typing them on your keyboard (the program will advance you to the next box automatically, but you can also use the arrow keys). After you've entered your answers, click the **Check My Answers** button to see how you've done.

Word Search: This game is not scored, but it is timed for your information. To play it, search for the words in the list on the right within the block of letters. When you find a word, click on the letters within it. The words can run horizontally, vertically, or diagonally.

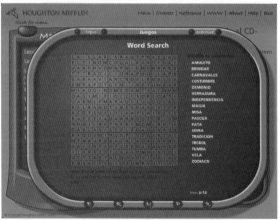

If your selection of letters is correct, the word in the word search list will be checked off.

Word Association Space Invader Game: In this game, you will see a group of spaceships labeled with words. Your goal is to detect and shoot the spaceship that is labeled with a word associated with a single theme before you are fired on. The theme is revealed upon the start of the game and can be reread by clicking on the **Mission Brief** button. To shoot the spaceship, use your mouse to place your cursor over the ship and click on it.

You will then be presented with a series of other spaceship groups, which you should handle in a similar manner. Your status is displayed in the middle of the screen. The music that accompanies the game can be turned on or off by clicking on the speaker icon.

Word Completion Maze: The objective of this game is to try and guess the hidden word. You must supply the letters to form the word. To start, click the word **Begin**. Where a hint is provided, click on the **Hint** button to receive a clue, then click on the letters that comprise the word the hint describes. For each instance of each correct letter, the frog in the maze will advance one gate.

For each incorrect letter, a block will be added to the exit. You must click on all the correct letters before the exit is blocked off and the frog is trapped in the maze.

Technical Support
For technical support, call Houghton Mifflin Software Support at 1-800-732-3223 between 9 a.m. and 5 p.m. EST Monday through Friday or email support@hmco.com.